Sleeping at School!

Story by Carmel Reilly
Illustrations by Susy Boyer

Contents

Chapter 1

A Note

Mitch came home from school
with a note.
There was going to be a sleepover camp
in the school hall.

"That will be a lot of fun, Mitch,"
said Mum.

"I can't wait," said Mitch,
with a big smile.

The day before the camp,
Mitch said to Mum,
“I don’t want to go to the sleepover.”

Mum was surprised.
“Why not?” she asked.

"Well ...," said Mitch. "What if I get scared? The hall is so big and dark."

"Lots of people will be there with you," said Mum.

Mitch was still not happy.

"I can pick you up after dinner,"
said Mum.
"Then you can have fun with your friends,
but you won't have to stay all night."

Mitch smiled.
"That would be good," he said.

Chapter 2

The Sleepover Camp

The next day was the sleepover camp.

After school, everyone met in the hall.

The children had something to eat.
Then, they played games outside.

Mitch saw Will sitting by himself.
Will was new at school.
He didn't have a lot of friends yet.

"Do you want to play a game with us?" Mitch asked Will.

"Yes, I do," said Will.

Chapter 3

A New Friend

At dinner time,
Mitch and Will sat together.

"This sleepover camp is fun
with you here!" said Will.

Just then, Mitch saw his mum.

"Mitch," she said. "Are you ready to go?"

Will looked sad.
"Are you going home now?" he asked.

"Mmm ...," said Mitch.
He looked up at Mum.

Mum smiled.
"You can stay if you want to," she said.

Mitch looked at Will.
"Would you like me to stay?"
he asked.

"Yes, please!" said Will.

Mitch looked at Mum again.
"Then I would like to stay, too,"
he said.

"I'll go home and get your things,"
said Mum.

Soon, Mum came back with Mitch's bag.
"I'm happy that you are going to stay,"
said Mum.

"Me too," said Will.

"Me too!" said Mitch.